THE MACMILLAN COMPANY, New York, New York / Collier-Macmillan Ltd., London

This book is for Alexa,

who is my daughter,
whose mother I am

JE

The art was prepared in pen and ink with an overlay for the green. The text is set in Linofilm Avant Garde Medium, the balloons in a variety of types.

On June 7
        my mother and father,
        who are my parents,
        whose daughter I am,
        and my brother,
        who is their son,
        whose sister I am,
        and I
        were just sitting down to lunch
                when the doorbell rang.

BZZZzz

My mother's parents,

who are my father's parents-in-law,
who are my grandparents,
whose granddaughter I am,

walked in.

My father's parents,

who are my mother's parents-in-law,
who are my grandparents,
whose granddaughter I am,

walked in.

Their son and daughter-in-law,

who are my father's brother and sister-in-law,
who are my mother's brother-in-law and sister-in-law,
who are my uncle and aunt,
whose niece I am,

walked in.

Their children,

> who are my grandparents' grandsons,
> who are my parents' nephews,
> who are my first cousins,
> whose first cousin I am,
>
> > hopped in.

My mother's sisters and their husbands,

who are my father's sisters-in-law and brothers-in-law,
who are my grandparents' daughters and sons-in-law,
who are my aunts and uncles,
whose niece I am,

walked in.

Their children,

who are my grandparents' granddaughters,
who are my parents' nieces,
who are my first cousins,
whose first cousin I am,

walked in.

Their great-grandmother,

who is my grandmother's mother,
who is my grandfather's mother-in-law,
who is my great-grandmother,
whose great-granddaughter I am,

hobbled in.

Her daughter and son-in-law,
      who are my grandmother's sister and brother-in-law,
      who are my mother's aunt and uncle,
      who are my great-aunt and great-uncle,
      whose great-niece I am,
                walked in.

Their daughter and her husband,

who is their son-in-law,

who are my grandparents' niece and nephew,

who are my mother's first cousins,

who are my second cousins,

whose second cousin I am,

walked in.

Their son,

who is my great-aunt's and great-uncle's grandson,
who is my mother's second cousin,
who is my third cousin,
whose third cousin I am,

crawled in.

We didn't fit at the table

so we went to the park and had a picnic.